You Can Do It, Sam

Amy Hest

illustrated by Anita Jeram

CANDLEWICK PRESS
CAMBRIDGE, MASSACHUSETTS

It happened one winter morning
on Plum Street . . .
and the moon was still up,
making moonbeams and
shadows on Plum Street.

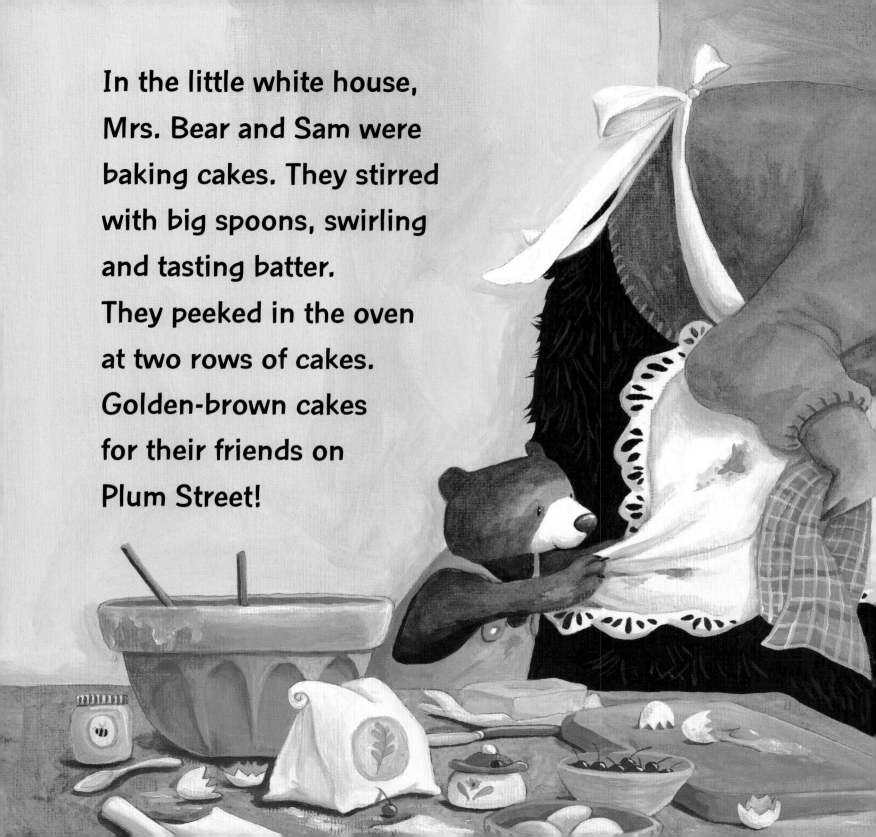

In the little white house,
Mrs. Bear and Sam were
baking cakes. They stirred
with big spoons, swirling
and tasting batter.
They peeked in the oven
at two rows of cakes.
Golden-brown cakes
for their friends on
Plum Street!

"Come on, cakes,"
whispered Sam.
"I can't wait,
I can't wait,
I can't wait!"

Mrs. Bear and Sam
waited for cakes.
"Now can we go, Mama?
Now?" said Sam.
"Soon," Mrs. Bear said.
"Soon, Sam."

They waited . . .
        and waited . . .
and then at last,
Mrs. Bear sniffed the air
with her nose in the air
and said, "I believe
our cakes are ready."

Mrs. Bear and Sam counted cakes, and there were twelve. They tucked them in bags, and there were twelve red bags.

Outside, snow tumbled on houses and sprinkled the trees.

It powdered the yard and Mrs. Bear's truck. Mrs. Bear and Sam climbed up in the truck that was green.

They bumped along in the early light.
Just the two of them on Plum Street,
uphill and down, up and down
to the very end of Plum Street.
"Our friends will love my cakes,"
Sam told his mama.
"Of course," Mrs. Bear said.

Mrs. Bear pulled up close
to the first sleepy house.
"Here we are, Sam. I'll wait here
and YOU take the cake."

"All by myself?" whispered Sam.

"Go, go, go!" Mrs. Bear put
her arm around Sam.

"You can do it, Sam."

And off he went.

All by himself in new snow.

All by himself,

waving a red bag and

waving to Mrs. Bear.

All by himself,

taking cake to their friends.

Sam left the red bag
at the door.
(The sign on the bag said:
A TASTY SURPRISE.)

Then he ran back to the truck, where his mama was waiting.

"I did it!" said Sam.

"Of course," Mrs. Bear said.

Mrs. Bear and Sam bumped along.

Just the two of them,

uphill and down, up and down.

At each sleepy house, Mrs. Bear

stopped the truck.

She put her arm around Sam.

"Here I go!" whispered Sam.
"Go, go, go!" Mrs. Bear said.
And off he went, making tracks
in new snow. Waving a red bag and
waving to Mrs. Bear. Leaving one
tasty cake at each sleepy door.

All by himself . . .

until they got home.

(There were TWO cakes left
in TWO red bags!)

"Hmmm," said Mrs. Bear.

"For us?" whispered Sam.

"Of course," Mrs. Bear said.

Mrs. Bear and Sam held hands on the path to the little white house . . .

and the sun was just sunning up
the little white house.
"Hello, house," said Sam, and they
went inside, kicking snow off their boots.

Mrs. Bear poured cocoa in cups and
they wriggled their toes in fat socks,
enjoying their cakes with cocoa.
As their bellies filled up,
they took turns telling stories.
Stories about a bear called Sam
who takes cakes (all by himself!)
to his friends . . . and they all love
his cakes so much!

And that's what happened.
One winter morning on Plum Street.

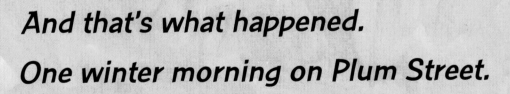

For Sam. Remember that day, that walk in deep snow, on Broadway?~A. H.
For Eileen—Queen of Cakes~A. J.

Text copyright © 2003 by Amy Hest
Illustrations copyright © 2003 by Anita Jeram

First edition in this form 2007

This edition published specially for Kohl's © 2007 by Candlewick Press, Inc.

Library of Congress Cataloging-in-Publication Data is available.
Library of Congress Catalog Card Number 2002034759

ISBN 978-0-7636-1934-3 (Trade edition)
ISBN 978-0-7636-3493-3 (Kohl's edition)

2 4 6 8 10 9 7 5 3 1

Printed in China

This book was typeset in Contemporary Brush Bold.
The illustrations were done in acrylic.

Candlewick Press
2067 Massachusetts Avenue
Cambridge, Massachusetts 02140

visit us at www.candlewick.com